MAIA
A DINOSAUR GROWS UP

By
John R. Horner and James Gorman

Illustrated by
Doug Henderson

Running Press
Philadelphia, Pennsylvania

This book was first published by the Museum of the Rockies, Montana
State University, Bozeman, Montana, in 1985, and edited by
Jeri D. Walton. Research for the book was funded in part by the Na-
tional Science Foundation.

Canadian representatives: General Publishing Co., Ltd., 30 Lesmill
Road, Don Mills, Ontario M3B 2T6
International representatives: Worldwide Media Services, Inc.
115 East Twenty-third Street, New York, New York 10010

9   8   7   6   5   4   3   2   1
The digit on the right indicates the number of this printing.

Library of Congress Cataloging-in-Publication Number 88-43384
ISBN 0-89471-691-3 (paper)
Jacket design by Toby Schmidt
Jacket illustration by Doug Henderson
Typography by Composing Room, Philadelphia, PA
Printed and bound in Hong Kong by South Sea Int'l Press Ltd.

This book may be ordered directly from the publisher. Please add
$1.50 for postage. *But try your bookstore first!* Running Press Book
Publishers, 125 South Twenty-second Street, Philadelphia,
Pennsylvania 19103

Contents

NOTE TO PARENTS AND TEACHERS

Dinosaurs were a very special and fascinating group of reptiles that lived as the dominant land animals during 140,000,000 years of earth history. Evidence of their presence on earth comes from their fossilized skeletal remains, footprints, and eggs. Paleontologists, such as myself, are able to make educated guesses as to what these animals looked like, what they ate, what kind of environments they lived in, and how they behaved, by studying their remains and the rocks in which they are found.

The story of Maia is fiction, but it is based on scientific information. We have recently discovered, in the state of Montana, fossilized nests, eggs, and baby and adult skeletons. As a scientist I formulate ideas or theories based on the kinds of fossil remains that I find. James Gorman, writer, has taken the scientific information and created this story. Doug Henderson, an exceptionally talented artist, has illustrated the story with paintings of scenes that I believe accurately depict our scientific information.

The story was written for young children because of their intense interest in these extinct animals. The study and interest in dinosaurs is often the first introduction to science for children, and unfortunately, in many instances, the information is out of date and inaccurate. It is my hope that by giving youngsters our most up-to-date information, they will continue to find an interest in this as well as other fields of science. I think it is important that they learn with us. I also believe it is important that they realize we do not have all the information, and that in time we may make discoveries which will change some of our ideas. Paleontologists are searching for the truth about dinosaurs. Along the way we may interpret some of the information incorrectly and have to rethink and revise some of our long-held theories. That is the way all of science is, and, since I don't expect we will ever have all the truths, that is the way it will continue.

—John R. Horner

Introduction

Eighty million years ago, duck-billed dinosaurs lived in what is now Montana. These dinosaurs laid eggs in nests and took care of their young babies, bringing them food. The dinosaur that lived that way is called Maiasaura (pronounced my-uh-SAWR-uh or mah-ee-uh-SAWR-uh). It has this name because Maiasaura means "Good Mother Lizard." This book is the story of what life was like for one of these Maiasaurs, whom we will call Maia (MY-uh or mah-EE-uh). Maia lived and died long before human beings existed.

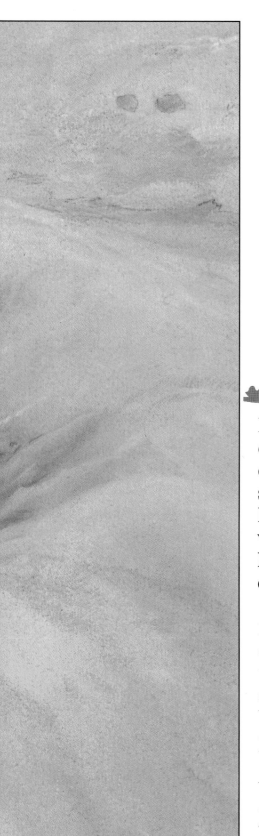

Out of the Egg

There were no clouds the day that Maia, the duck-billed dinosaur came out of her egg. The sun beat down on the hot dry ground. It shone on the nest of dinosaur eggs. The mother dinosaur had laid her eggs on the ground, and covered them with leaves and twigs. Even under the leaves, inside the eggs, the baby dinosaurs could feel the sun.

Inside Maia's egg, it was dark. Maia felt that she had to stretch. Although the egg was as big as a grapefruit, it was getting too small for Maia. She was a foot and a half long. She was curled up in a tight ball—too tight. She started to squirm, and peep and squeak.

Her mother, who was 30 feet long and weighed two tons, put her head down low over the nest and listened to the sounds. Then she scraped the leaves off the eggs to let the sun shine on them.

Suddenly, it was light inside Maia's egg. Maia didn't know what light was, or what the sun was, because she had always been inside the egg, but the light made her want to get out of the egg even more.

She began to bang her nose on the shell, jerking her head up and down. On the tip of her nose was something like a tooth. It would wear out and fall off after she had hatched, but for now it was useful. She banged it against the egg with all of her strength.

Finally the egg cracked. Then a bigger crack appeared. Soon the whole top came off, and Maia, the baby dinosaur, climbed out into the sun to get her first look at the world.

She was mostly grey, and looked like a big lizard. She had a red mark on both sides of her back that made her look different from her brothers and sisters.

She was also different because she was the first one in her nest to break out of the egg.

As soon as Maia tried to move she fell, as all babies do. The first thing she stumbled into was another baby dinosaur, just like herself, coming out of an egg. The next thing she did was step on an egg and break the top. That was all right because another baby was trying to hatch out of that egg. When Maia caved in his roof it just helped him along.

Wherever Maia turned, there were more dinosaurs, all her own size, and all just as awkward. Each had just hatched or was right in the middle of hatching. By the end of the day that Maia hatched, all the other eggs had hatched, too. There were twenty squeaking, tumbling, little baby dinosaurs.

All around their nest were other nests, each on top of a mound of dirt. Each nest was six feet wide and scooped out of the ground so that it was shaped like a salad bowl. There were two hundred nests, all filled with baby dinosaurs.

The mother dinosaurs who had laid the eggs stayed by the nests or went to the banks of the nearby stream to gather food. There were berry bushes by the stream, and in it fish waved their tails, alligators hunted, and turtles on logs lay basking in the sun.

Maia didn't know anything about the other dinosaurs or the turtles and the stream. She couldn't even see over the edge of her nest. All she knew was that she was hungry. Of course, she didn't know exactly what being hungry was, since she had never needed to eat before. She just felt so empty that she squeaked. It was such a loud squeak that it knocked her down. She was surprised that noises that loud could come out of her.

She felt hungry again, so she stood up and squeaked again. All the other babies were doing it too. Soon, it seemed like the most natural thing to do, to squeak and squeak, and make a noise that would send a human mother running out the door.

That isn't what Maia's mother did. She came right over to the nest. Maia looked up and saw an enormous reddish brown creature with a mouth that looked like a duck's bill. The bill was full of berries. As Maia watched and squeaked, her mother bent down and dropped the berries from her mouth. Maia wasn't frightened. She was a dinosaur, so her mother looked just right, big and red, with a mouth full of berries.

Maia smelled her mother's mouth, and then she sniffed the berries. They smelled so good she grabbed them in her mouth and started crunching them between her teeth. They tasted so good she grabbed more and ate them. So did the other babies. The only thing on Maia's mind was berries. She pushed and shoved on her unsteady legs like a greedy puppy, trying to eat every berry in the nest.

Soon the feeling that made her squeak stopped. She wasn't hungry anymore. She stopped eating, and she stopped squeaking. The sun was beating down on her, and it was hot.

She closed her eyes and went to sleep. It had been a very big day.

A Scary Day

The next day, and the day after that, went along in the same way. Maia never left the nest. She and her brothers and sisters slept, and squeaked, and ate. Their mother brought them nuts and berries from the bushes that grew on the banks of the nearby stream. Maia's father sometimes came by the nest too. He prowled around the nesting ground and smelled all the babies, even the ones that weren't his own.

As the days passed, Maia grew. She was the quickest of the babies in her nest, and she was usually first to snatch a berry when it fell in the nest. Some of her brothers and sisters were bigger than she was and some were smaller. One had bumpy skin on his nose. Another had a crooked leg and a crooked tail. He had come out of the egg that way. Maia was the only one with red patches on her back.

One day, as Maia was about to fall asleep in the sun, she heard screaming and honking from the adult dinosaurs. She was big enough now to see over the edge of the nest and she saw a pack of red dinosaurs the size of wolves running through the nesting ground.

They were *Troödon*.

Maia squeaked and screamed with

the other babies as the pack ran by. The adult duckbills were chasing them. Maia saw that one *Troödon* had a baby from another nest in his mouth.

The duckbills became quiet as soon as the pack of *Troödon* ran from the nesting ground. Life went back to normal. Maia slept. She woke up. She tried to push Crooked Leg out of the nest. He pushed back hard because even with his bad leg he was strong and both of them tumbled over the other babies.

A few days later the pack of *Troödon* came again. When the screaming and honking started, Maia and her brothers and sisters squeaked for help, but their mother was off in the woods. The *Troödon* pack ran right at Maia's nest.

One *Troödon* stopped at the edge. He had a long, toothy head at the end of a snake-like neck. He scared Maia so much she wanted to run as fast as she could, but she was afraid to leave the nest. It was the only place that she knew. The babies were afraid to run, and they were afraid to stay, so they just squeaked and crowded toward the far end of the nest. The *Troödon* moved fast. His head shot forward, and his jaws snapped shut on the biggest duckbill in the nest. He snatched him up and ran away to eat him.

The screaming soon died down, because the *Troödon* pack had escaped. Maia and her brothers and sisters calmed down. They forgot right away about the baby that was gone. That wasn't because they were mean or cruel. It's just that they were dinosaurs. Someone in the herd would always be getting caught and killed by meat-eaters. They would always forget and get on with what they were doing. But there was one thing Maia did not forget. That was the *Troödon*. As long as she lived, whenever she saw a *Troödon*, she would know he was an enemy.

Leaving the Nest

The packs of *Troödon* came often to the nesting ground. Other babies were snatched from Maia's nest, and two became sick and died. One rolled over the edge and down the side just as an adult was walking by, and was crushed. Maia survived because she was quick and lucky. Most of her time she spent eating, and growing.

Maia grew so fast she almost split her skin. By the time she was only five months old, she was three feet long. Her brothers and sisters had grown too. They were changing color. Their bills were wider and longer. They were all so big that they could barely fit in the nest. When their mother brought food, they all jumped and rushed for the berries.

It was so crowded, Maia was always finding some other baby's foot or tail in her mouth. One day, she was in such a hurry eating berries that she didn't notice

that she had caught Crooked Leg's tail in her mouth. She bit down hard, and he screeched and whirled around and tumbled her over the edge of the nest. Of course, she scrambled right back. Even though the nest was crowded, none of the babies wanted to be out of it. They wanted to stay in the nest, and eat.

They got what they wanted, until the day their mother didn't bring any food. This set off an awful racket of squeaking and honking among Maia and her brothers and sisters. All day passed and a night too, and still no food came. The next morning Maia's mother showed her head over the edge of the nest. All the young dinosaurs expected berries. Instead they got a surprise. Their mother stuck her bill in the nest and tumbled three babies out of the nest with one push. Maia got caught the second time. She came rolling down the outside of the nest, did a somersault, and landed on her head. By the time she could sit up straight and look around her, all the other young dinosaurs were out of the nest, sitting on the ground.

Maia had plenty of room now, but it was scary. Her mother looked bigger than ever. There were adults almost ten times Maia's size, all around her. There was no comfortable nest to protect her.

As if all this weren't scary enough, her mother started walking away. All the young dinosaurs squeaked and honked, but Maia's mother kept on walking. Soon she would be gone and the young dinosaurs would be all alone, and outside the

nest. Nothing like this had ever happened before, and Maia wasn't going to let it happen now.

She didn't wait an extra second. She got up on her feet and ran after her mother. Crooked Leg was next, and their brothers and sisters followed. They all kept squeaking and honking with all their might.

Maia's mother walked right out of the nesting ground with her whole family chasing after her. She walked and walked, and Maia and the other youngsters got more and more hungry.

Maia's mother didn't stop until they came to some round, tall bushes full of the plump berries Maia had eaten in the nest. She had never seen them on a bush before. She had never seen a bush.

Maia's mother dropped her head to the bush. She closed her mouth on the branches, and she pulled back, ripping off leaves, twigs, berries, and all. Maia and the others crowded around their mother, waiting to be fed.

To their surprise, she ate all the berries herself. While Maia and the other young dinosaurs honked and squeaked around her, she crushed the berries and leaves with her teeth, and swallowed them. Only a drop or two of berry juice ran down from her chin and fell on the babies at her feet.

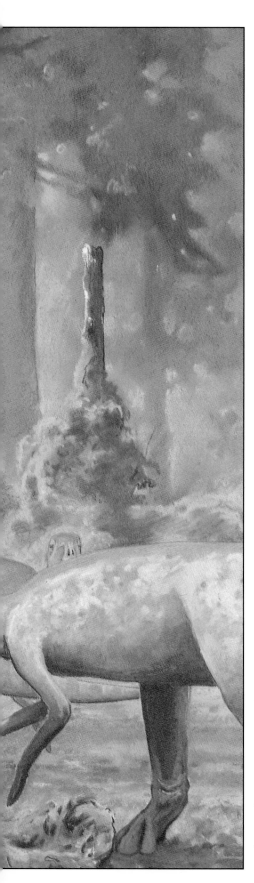

That was too much for Maia. She was too hungry to wait. She went over to the bush and bit on a low branch.

She got only a few berries the first time, so she tried again. The next time she got more.

Her brothers and sisters did the same. All of them bit and tore the berry bushes. Maia was very happy to feed on the bushes.

Once she was full, she waded into the nearby stream, and drank. Being in the water was like getting wet in the rain, except there was so much water.

She came out of the stream feeling ready for a nap, but just as she was about to lie down on a warm rock that she had picked out, her mother walked off again. The rest of the family had to follow, and Maia had to run to keep up.

A Long Trip

Maia lived with her family near the mountains for a year. She learned to live outside the nest. Maia's mother taught her and her brothers and sisters all the good things to eat. Maia learned where the berry bushes were, where the streams were, and where the best places to sleep were. She also learned to stay away from the meat-eating dinosaurs who were always trying to catch duckbills.

By the time the year was over, Maia was fifteen feet long and weighed 750 pounds. She wasn't a baby any longer, nor were her brothers and sisters. Only eight of them had survived. Luckily, Crooked Leg was one of them. As he had grown, his leg had gotten stronger. He was never quite as quick as Maia, but he was quick enough.

At the end of the year, all the families began to come together. Each day more dinosaurs came to join the great herd. Soon there were hundreds of dinosaurs.

They raised clouds of dust when they walked. They stripped trees bare when they ate. They made a noise like an earthquake when they ran. Maia had never seen so many dinosaurs.

Once the herd was together, it began a journey. Slowly, each day, the herd moved east. Each day, bit by bit, the land grew greener. Maia didn't know what was happening, but the older dinosaurs did. The herd was leaving the nesting place, where the ground was dry and good for nests. They were traveling down to the lowlands, on the edge of a great sea.

It took a month for the herd to travel 100 miles. When they stopped, they were in a place that was like nothing Maia had ever seen. There were trees and bushes and water all around. Different kinds of green plants grew everywhere that Maia looked. No brown dust from the dry earth got in Maia's nose. The land was wet and warm and full of good things to eat.

Maia learned to eat new kinds of trees, and bushes, and water plants. Sometimes she waded into ponds and swamps and pulled up lush green plants with her bill.

There were many dinosaurs that Maia had never seen before. There were ankylosaurs, with clubs on their tails. There were dinosaurs like monoclonius, with long horns and hard skin. There were other duckbills. There were lots of meat-eaters.

The biggest and most dangerous kind of meat-eater was called *Albertosaurus*. The albertosaurs were 30 feet long, with huge heads and long, sharp teeth.

Maia knew that she should always be watching for meat-eaters, but there was so much new, delicious food that sometimes she forgot.

One day she was chewing the leaves of a soft swamp tree. It was so good that she wasn't thinking about anything else. As she bent for a low branch she heard a loud sucking noise behind her. She turned and saw an albertosaur lifting his foot from the mud.

He began to charge, and as he came close she could hear his teeth click. Maia was as scared as she had been when the *Troödons* attacked her nest, but now she was bigger, and faster, and she knew she had to get away.

She turned and ran, splashing in the muddy pond. She was lighter than the albertosaur and the mud did not slow her down as much as it did him. He leaped forward to catch her, but instead of closing his jaws on her leg, he fell face first into the muddy water. Maia kept running, as fast as she could, and she didn't stop until she found her family. She had learned an old lesson once again. No matter how quick she was, she still had to be careful. She could never have a relaxed meal. Like all the other duckbills who wanted to stay alive, while she was eating, she had to look around her every half-minute to make sure that no other dinosaur was about to eat her.

Good
Mother
Maia

In the lowlands Maia grew big, and she grew up. One year, the dinosaurs in Maia's herd gathered to go back to the nesting ground, near the mountains. They were going to make nests and raise babies. Maia's mother went with the herd.

Maia and her brothers and sisters were all too young to make their own nests, so they stayed in the lowlands.

Maia began to spend all of her time with Crooked Leg and two of her sisters. Together they explored the land near the sea. Once they went right to the shore.

Maia waded in the ocean and started to drink. The water was so salty it almost made her sick, so they traveled back to the ponds and swamps they knew.

A second time the herd gathered to go back to the nesting ground, but still Maia didn't go. She was still too young to be a mother.

When the herd gathered for the third time, Maia felt different. She was now 30 feet long and weighed two tons. She was as big as her mother had been. It was time for her to be a mother too.

She joined the herd with Crooked Leg and her sisters. They all made the trip to the nesting ground. In a month they came to the high dry land near the mountains. Here Maia could lay her eggs safely. In the wet ground in the lowlands the eggs would have rotted and never hatched.

When they reached the nesting ground Maia picked a good spot. With her powerful hind legs she scratched up dirt to make a mound. Then, with her short arms she hollowed it out at the top. The nest was six feet across, and shaped like a salad bowl.

Maia waited near her nest for a mate. Several male duckbills with long fringes down their backs would come and parade around her. They would bellow at each other, and show off their fringes so that they looked big and strong. Maia picked the one with the best fringe. He was her mate. The other males had to find other females.

Maia laid 25 eggs. She poked each of them into the ground and covered them with leaves to keep them warm. Even though Maia had never made a nest before, she knew what to do. And she did it all herself. Her mate was busy eating, or prowling around the nesting ground. Maia was very careful about her eggs. She watched over them and tried to keep lizards away from them. She was not alone as she waited for them to hatch. Hundreds of other female dinosaurs, just like her, did exactly the same thing.

One day, near her nest, Maia heard a faint squeak, almost like a bird chirping, but there were no birds nearby. She lowered her head just above the nest, just as her mother had once done. She listened carefully, and she heard one squeak, and then another, from babies still inside their eggs. She pulled the leaves and twigs off the eggs, and let the sun shine on them.

She waited, and after a while, one egg cracked. Next the top was pushed off, and a tiny nose poked up out of the egg. Out came the baby dinosaur into the sunlight. It stumbled, as all babies do. Then another came out, and another, and the squeaking got louder.

Maia went off to the berry bushes where she had first learned to gather her own food. With one bite she swept a basketful of berries into her mouth. She carried them back and dumped them in the nest, and watched all the little babies fall over each other to get them.

Every day Maia went to gather berries. Every day she kept away from the big meat-eaters. Every day she saw packs of *Troödon* running through the nesting ground and sometimes she chased them.

One day just as Maia returned from the berry bushes, she saw a *Troödon* at the edge of her own nest. She dropped the berries from her mouth and they rolled all over the ground.

She let out a great blast of noise that made every dinosaur on the nesting ground look at her. Even the *Troödon* stopped, and looked up. That was a mistake. By the time he saw Maia running toward him, it was too late for him to escape, and he was too small to fight Maia.

Maia stepped right on the *Troödon*. She had powerful legs and she caught him with one foot before he could move. Her foot crushed him. She kept bringing her foot down on the *Troödon* until his body rolled down the side of the nest in a limp heap.

Maia waited, and watched the *Troödon* to see if he would move. She sniffed him. When she was sure he was dead she pushed him farther away from the nest.

She got more berries and gave
them to the nestlings, who squeaked with
delight.

Maia was happy too, because she had
saved her babies. There would be other
dangers, later on, but not right now. Maia
had done her job well, even though it was
her first nest.

Maia was a good mother dinosaur.

Glossary

Albertosaurus (al-ber-tuh-SAWR-us): A meat-eating dinosaur that stood about 8 feet tall at the hips, and weighed about 3 tons. Its remains have been found in Alberta, Canada; Montana; and Wyoming. Albertosaurs were related to the tyrannosaurs.

Ankylosaur (an-KY-lo-sawr): A plant-eating dinosaur that walked on all fours and grew to about 20 feet in length. The tip of its tail was bony and club-shaped.

Dinosaur (DI-no-sawr): A common name meaning "terrible lizard" that was given to two groups of extinct reptiles (ornithischians and saurischians) that were closely related to birds.

Duck-billed dinosaur: A common name given to the hadrosaurs because of their duck-like beaks. There were many varieties of duck-billed dinosaurs, some of which had hollow crests on the tops of their heads. Duck-billed dinosaurs, or hadrosaurs, have been found all over the world, and were probably the most common kind of dinosaur. Duck-bills ate plants and were probably the only reptiles that chewed their food.

Maiasaura (my-uh-SAWR-uh or mah-ee-uh-SAWR-uh): A kind of duck-billed dino-saur, or hadrosaur, found in western Montana. *Maiasaura* means "good mother lizard." Newly hatched maiasaurs were only 14 inches long and weighed about 1½ lbs. Full grown, they were about 30 feet in length and weighed around 3 tons.

Monoclonius (mon-o-CLONE-ee-us): A horned dinosaur found in Montana and Alberta. Full grown it was about 20 feet long and weighed around 2½ tons. *Monoclonius*, like all of the horned dinosaurs, ate plants.

Paleontologist (pail-e-on-TALL-o-jist): A scientist who studies the remains of extinct or fossil life. A vertebrate paleontologist studies fossil animals that have skeletons, whereas an invertebrate paleontologist studies animals that lack bones. A scientist who studies fossil plants is called a paleobotanist or a botan-ical paleontologist.

"The Sea": In this story Maia and her brothers and sisters go to a sea which existed in the middle of North America. The sea connected the Gulf of Mexico with the Arctic Ocean during the time of dinosaurs. This warm sea has been named the Western Interior Cretaceous Seaway.

Troödon (TRUE-o-don): A small meat-eating dinosaur that probably grew no larger than 6 feet in length. The teeth of *Troödon* are found commonly in the areas where the maiasaurs nested, suggesting that they may have eaten baby dinosaurs.